NINJA KID 11

NINJA ARTISTS!

Scholastic Press
An imprint of Scholastic Australia Pty Limited (ABN 11 000 614 577)
PO Box 579 Gosford NSW 2250
www.scholastic.com.au

Part of the Scholastic Group
Sydney • Auckland • New York • Toronto • London • Mexico City
• New Delhi • Hong Kong • Buenos Aires • Puerto Rico

First published by Scholastic Australia in 2023.
Text copyright © Anh Do, 2023.
Illustrations by Anton Emdin and Jeremy Ley, 2023.
The moral rights of Anh Do have been asserted.
The moral rights of Anton Emdin and Jeremy Ley have been asserted.

ISBN 978 1 76120 244 5

 A catalogue record for this
book is available from the
NATIONAL
LIBRARY National Library of Australia
OF AUSTRALIA

Typeset in Bizzle-Chizzle, featuring Hola Bisou and Handblock.

Printed in China by RR Donnelley.
Scholastic Australia's policy, in association with RR Donnelley, is to use
papers that are renewable and made efficiently from wood grown in
responsibly managed forests, so as to minimise its environmental footprint.

10 9 8 7 6 5 4 3 2   23 24 25 26 27 / 2

ANH DO

illustrated by Anton Emdin

NiNJA KiD 11

NINJA ARTISTS!

A Scholastic Press book
from Scholastic Australia

ONE

Hi, I'm Nelson Kane.
Most of the time, I'm an **ordinary**
kid.

But whenever trouble turns up, I transform into **NiNJA KiDI!**

I live in a junkyard with my mum, Grandma and my cousin Kenny, otherwise known as **H-DUDE**, my always-hungry sidekick.

Kenny and I go to school together, and today the teacher announced the coolest thing ever . . . an *Art Contest!*

Kenny and I **love** art, and we love a competition. We couldn't wait to get started!

Our teacher, Mr Fletcher, introduced us to a professional artist who was going to run the contest.

His name was

Mocasso!

Mocasso asked us to **pair up** for the contest. You won't believe who I chose as my partner . . .

CHARLES, THE CLASS BULLY!

Just kidding! I paired up with Kenny, of course!

'Now you've chosen your partners,' Mocasso said, 'it's time to make **beautiful** art!'

Mocasso waved his hand around as though he was **painting** the air.

'Can I paint my pet **llama?**' Billy Bob asked. 'He has a prettier face than the Mona Lisa.'

'No-one has a **prettier** face than the Mona Lisa!' Mocasso snapped. 'And you will not be painting llamas, you'll be painting FANTASTICAL, MYTHICAL CREATURES!'

'Your artworks will feature in an art **exhibition** at the Town Hall,' Mocasso said.

'The Town Hall?' I exclaimed. 'That's **epic!**'

'Is there a prize for the best painting?' Tiffany asked.

'**Cold hard cash?**' Charles asked.

'Hamburger vouchers?' Kenny enquired.

'The prize is far more **valuable** than those things,' Mocasso said. 'It will be a surprise.'

Riiiiiing!!!

The school bell rang and we packed up our things.

'You must choose your MYTHICAL CREATURE by tomorrow morning,' Mocasso said. 'Think **BIG.** Dream **BIG.** Inspire me!'

TWO

That night, Kenny and I asked Mum and Grandma for MYTHICAL BEAST suggestions while we were eating dinner.

As usual, Kenny was on to his **third** serving, while the rest of us were still on our first!

Did I mention that Kenny is ALWAYS hungry?

'What about a **dragon**?' Grandma asked.

'Or a **griffin,**' Mum said. 'I've always had a soft spot for griffins.'

'Ah, griffins,' Kenny said knowingly.
'The front legs and head of a **lion,** and
the back legs of an **eagle.**'

'Close,' Mum replied. 'Just everything
you said . . . in **reverse.**'

'I like my version better,' Kenny said.

Griffin

Kenny's
version

'Or you could paint a **unicorn**,'
Grandma said.

'Or a **Pegasus**,' Mum said.

'Or a **werewolf**,' Grandma added.

'At first, we had no ideas,' I said. 'Now we've got so many I can't decide.'

'We need a sign,' Kenny said. 'Any sign.'

DING DONG!

It was the doorbell.

The sign!' Kenny exclaimed as we raced to the door.

Kenny and I were so **excited** that we opened the door at the same time! We weren't disappointed. It was our **favourite** visitor . . . Patty the Post Lady!

'Hey, Patty!' I said.

'Which mythical creature do you think we should **paint** for our school art competition?' Kenny blurted out.

'I don't know much about mythical creatures,' Patty said. 'But I know I have a **package** for you both!'

NELSON
& KENNY
DUCK CREEK

'Yes!' I exclaimed. 'I **love** packages!'

'Especially when they're addressed to us,' Kenny added.

'Thanks, Patty!' we said in unison.

Kenny and I couldn't wait, we ripped open the package on the spot! If we were excited before, now we were **SUPER EXCITED.** It was the latest *Pow Pow Pig* book!

We ran back to Grandma and Mum.

'Which one of you **wonderful** humans bought us the new *Pow Pow* book?' I asked.

'Because you're about to get a **HUGE** Kenny hug!' Kenny added.

'Not me,' Grandma said.

'Me either,' Mum said.

'Perhaps it was a ΜΥΤΗΙϹΑL CREATURE?' suggested Grandma.

'Whoever it was,' Kenny said, 'is my new **favourite** person.'

'Do you think it's **OK** to take a break from **BRAINSTORMING** mythical creatures so we can read our new book?' I asked Mum.

'It's always a **yes** from me if it's about reading,' Mum said.

'Thank you, thank you, thank you!' Kenny shouted excitedly.

We **RUSHED** to our room as fast as our legs would carry us.

Kenny and I were so excited about the new *Pow Pow* book that we decided to **dress up** as our favourite characters to read it!

'We're looking pretty good,' Kenny said. 'But it just feels like we need a little something **extra** . . .'

After trying on a variety of accessories, we settled on our **underwater breathing necklaces.**

'They look great!' Kenny exclaimed.

The book had us **hooked** from the very first page with twists, turns and awesome jokes.

When we stopped reading to take a breath, Kenny asked, 'Remember when we zapped a *Pow Pow* book with Grandma's **Character Camera,** and Pow Pow and the gang joined us in our world?'

'How could I **forget**,' I replied.

Kenny plucked Grandma's Character Camera off the shelf. 'Should we try it again?!' he mused.

'**Definitely not!**' I replied. 'Remember what Grandma said – it's only to be used in **emergencies**.'

'Yeah, yeah,' Kenny said, sighing as he stared into the camera.

'Be **careful** with that,' I warned.

'**Relax!**' Kenny exclaimed, looking closer at the Character Camera. 'I'm not going to set it to–

Kenny pressed the button!

The next thing we knew, Kenny and I were **falling from the sky!**

THREE

'**A**hhhhhhh!'
    Kenny and I screamed for our lives as we **plummeted** through the clouds. As the ground drew closer, we closed our eyes, certain we were about to become as **flat as pancakes!**

Kenny and I were

falling . . .
falling . . .
falling. Then not falling.

Someone had caught us! We opened
our eyes and couldn't believe what we
were seeing. I was in the arms of Pow Pow
Pig. And Kenny had been caught by Barry
the Goat!

'I never knew I had an **identical twin!**' Barry said, looking shocked.

'Not quite. It's not your twin,' Pow Pow said. 'Don't you recognise these little **legends?**'

Barry smiled. 'Nelson! Kenny! Is that really you?! I have to say, Kenny, you are **looking gooooood!**'

Before we could respond, the Character Camera **dropped** out of the sky.

'Be back in one second!' I yelled as Kenny and I **RACED** to catch it.

I was perfectly positioned to catch the Character Camera when it **smacked** into the branch of a large peach tree and **dropped** towards the lake. Kenny and I hurried over to the lake only to watch in horror as a **massive head** emerged from the water and took the Character Camera!

The **ENORMOUS** creature smiled playfully then **disappeared** underwater.

'**What on earth was that?!**' Kenny asked.

'No idea,' I said. 'But we really **need** to get the Character Camera back!'

As I prepared to dive into the water, Kenny stared at me in **disbelief.** 'Are you really diving in to go after that creature?'

'It's our only way home!' I replied and dived in.

Kenny reluctantly **followed** me.

GULP!

The lake was **deep** and **dark** and we could only just make out the creature, a **long way** in front of us.

When it realised we were chasing it, it turned around and **winked!** Then it swam off so quickly, Kenny and I had no chance of catching up to it.

Kenny and I climbed out of the water, **horrified** that we'd lost the Character Camera.

Pow Pow, Cha Cha, Barry and Kung Fu were waiting for us at the edge of the lake.

'What are you two doing here?' Kung Fu asked.

'It's a **Surprise** visit!' Kenny said. 'Meaning we're just as surprised as you that we're here!'

'We **accidentally** zapped ourselves with the Character Camera,' I said.

'It was all **my fault,**' Kenny said as he stared sadly at the ground.

'It was a total accident,' I said to Kenny. 'But we need to get the Character Camera back from that **strange monster** or we won't be able to get home.'

'**Ever!**' Kenny added, his face worried.

'We know all about not being able to get home,' Pow Pow said sadly.

'We'll **help** you boys find your Character zapper thingy,' Cha Cha added.

42

'At least we can get out of these wet costumes now,' Kenny said, starting to rip off his dripping Barry the Goat outfit.

'That's **not** a good idea,' Pow Pow said.

'The animals here will **freak** if they see a couple of humans roaming around,' Kung Fu said.

'It's best that you **pretend** to be one of us!' Cha Cha said.

'So, where **exactly** are we?' I asked.

'We're in Scotland,' Kung Fu said. 'In the **year** 1840!'

'**Whoa!**' Kenny exclaimed.

'I can't believe we're in the **PAST**,' I said.

'You get used to it,' said Cha Cha.

'Although the food's not always great,' Barry said. 'Which reminds me, I'm **soooooo hungry**.'

'Me too!' said Kenny.

'Guys!' Kung Fu exclaimed. 'We need to **focus** on getting the Character Camera back.'

'Excellent idea,' Pow Pow said. 'But the lake is **ENORMOUS.** The monster could be anywhere.'

We should ask a local for advice!

The six of us **wandered** around the
outside of the lake until we reached a sign.

East Loch was closer, and the sign looked **friendlier,** so we walked as quickly as our legs would take us towards the **East Castle.**

FOUR

When we reached East Loch Castle, there was a fight happening outside the castle walls.

Animals were **cheering** and **booing** as six scrawny squirrels battled six even **scrawnier rats!**

In the end, the rats **scurried** away, leaving the squirrels victorious.

'Congratulations to the
swashbuckling squirrels,'
a regal-looking deer with her right
arm in a sling announced. 'These **brave
warriors** will represent East Castle in
tomorrow's **GRAND BATTLE.'**

The crowd didn't seem overly **excited** about being represented by six scrawny squirrels.

'Bravo, Duchess!' a rabbit standing next to the deer exclaimed, trying to rev up the crowd.

BRAVO!

As the crowd dispersed, I looked to Pow Pow and the others. 'Who should we ask about the **Lake Monster?**'

'That rabbit seems to know what's going on,' Pow Pow said. He pointed to the rabbit who was stepping out of the castle.

We hurried over to the rabbit. He looked closely at me and **wrinkled his nose.**

'You are a very **strange-looking** pig,' he said.

'I'm a **rare** breed,' I replied awkwardly.

Kenny shuffled **nervously** as the rabbit looked him up and down. 'You are one *handsome* goat,' the rabbit said.

'I agree,' Barry said.

I try and stay in shape!

'Why haven't I seen you animals before?' the rabbit asked.

'We're **travellers!**' Pow Pow said.

'Oh!' the rabbit said, his mood dramatically changing. 'We **welcome** travellers with open arms in East Loch. My name is Robert. Would you like to meet the **Duchess?**'

'We'd **love to** meet the Duchess,' Pow Pow said. 'But first, we need to find the Lake Monster.'

'Nessie?' Robert said.

'Nessie?' the six of us enquired.

'**Beautiful Nessie,** the Loch Ness monster,' Robert replied. 'You won't find her now, she'll be **resting** at the bottom of the lake.'

'Oh,' I exclaimed, disappointed.

'You might have **more luck** in the morning,' Robert said.

'Maybe we can meet the Duchess in the meantime,' Cha Cha said hopefully, and Robert led us into the castle.

When we reached the balcony, the Duchess was looking down nervously at the courtyard where the **scrawny squirrels** were training for the big battle.

As soon as Robert introduced us to the Duchess, her face softened. She was **super cool!**

She fed us tasty snacks and told us all about the annual **battle** between the East and West Castles.

'The **winning castle** gets to decide the fate of the Loch Ness monster,' the Duchess said.

'Decide her fate?' Pow Pow said. 'What does that mean?'

'We want her to be **free** to roam the lake,' the Duchess said. 'But the villagers of the West Castle want to hunt her.'

We gasped in **horror.**

'I can safely say I hate the West Loch Castle,' Cha Cha said.

'Fortunately,' the Duchess continued,
'my castle **always** wins.'

'Really?' I said, shooting a look down at the **scrawny** squirrels.

'That's because we usually have the Duchess fighting for us,' Robert said. 'She's the most **gifted** sword-wielder in the land.'

'I can't fight this year because I hurt my shoulder doing too many one-armed **push-ups,'** the Duchess said, shaking her head. 'I really should have stopped at one thousand.'

6001 . . .
6002 . . .
6003 . . .

'Without the Duchess's leadership,' Robert continued, 'our usual warriors were **too scared** to fight. So we had to arrange a competition to see who would represent us.'

'And those squirrels won?' Cha Cha said.

'Yep,' the Duchess said, glancing at the squirrels again. 'There **wasn't** a lot of competition.'

One of the squirrels accidentally **whacked** himself in the head with a club.

'Excuse me, Duchess,' I said. 'If we wanted to find the Loch Ness monster, where would we look?'

'Sightings are rare,' the Duchess said. 'But Nessie always pops up her head on the **first full moon** of spring.'

'When's that?' I asked eagerly.

'Tomorrow night,' the Duchess replied. 'It's my favourite night of the year . . . if we win the battle, of course. Anyway, I think it's time we all got some rest. Tomorrow promises to be a **HUGE** day.'

We slept in the castle's **ENORMOUS** guest room. The pillows were so soft it was like sleeping on clouds.

'I could get used to this **royal** treatment,' yawned Kenny, getting ready

for bed. 'You have to admit, King Kenny has a nice ring to it!'

Even though we were far from home, Kenny and I had the **best** sleep we'd had in ages.

FiVE

Next morning, we gathered at a clearing near the lake to watch the **battle.** It was like a football final with villagers chanting, singing and waving flags.

WEST IS BEST

WE ♥ CONAN

GO THE EAST BEASTS

SAMMY SQUIRREL YOU'RE MY HERO!

go CONAN!

Suddenly, a **meerkat** in a pink suit and sunglasses ran into the clearing.

'That is one cool-looking meerkat!' I said.

'The coolest in the business!' Robert said. 'That's **Anna the Announcer.**'

ARE YOU READY TO RUMBLE?!

For a tiny animal, her voice was **ENORMOUS.** The crowd went **NUTS!**

Anna introduced the **WEST CASTLE WARRIORS,** a massive team consisting of a rhino, a hyena, a gorilla, a wolf, a crazy-looking raccoon and a **HUGE** lizard.

'They look **seriously scary!**' I whispered to Kenny.

'Especially that rhino!' Kenny said.

'That's Conan,' Robert said. 'The **DUKE** of West Castle.'

'Now it's time to meet the **EAST CASTLE GLADIATORS!**' Anna said.

The six scrawny squirrels stumbled into the arena, and the East Castle villagers cheered. But they were wasting their breath. As soon as the squirrels saw their opponents, **they panicked!**

The squirrels' eyes were bulging more than the rhino's muscles! They **SPRINTED** out of the clearing and **fled into the forest!**

'The East Castle Gladiators have **left** the arena,' Anna announced. 'This is a **forfeit,** which means the fate of the Loch Ness monster rests in the West Castle Warriors' giant hands.'

The West Castle Warriors raised their arms in victory. Their villagers shouted,

'Hunt the monster! Hunt the monster!'

'We can't let them **hunt** that beautiful creature,' Cha Cha said.

'**Definitely not!**' I replied.

'How do we stop them?' Kenny asked.

'The six of us must **represent** East Castle,' Pow Pow said.

'**Ah . . . what?!**' Barry shrieked. He seemed on the verge of fainting.

'Every **good deed** makes the future a little brighter,' Cha Cha said.

'That's your motto!' Kenny said.

'Sure is,' Kung Fu said. 'What do you think, boys? Are you in?'

I pulled Kenny away from the others. 'We need to stay in these costumes,' I whispered. 'Which means we can't become Ninja Kid and H-Dude.'

'You have your **ninja powers,** but I'll have to fight those beasts . . . **as plain old Kenny?!**' Kenny asked nervously.

'We won't be alone,' I said. 'We'll be fighting alongside our **heroes!**'

Kenny looked across to Pow Pow, Cha Cha, Barry and Kung Fu.

You're right. I'm in!

Robert had overheard our discussion.
'You can't represent East Castle,' he said.
'You don't live here.'

'Is that the only way we're **allowed** to
compete?' Pow Pow asked.

'Unless you get **special permission**
from the Duchess,' Robert said.

'Then what are we **waiting for?!**'
Pow Pow said. **'Let's go!'**

We found the Duchess in the castle, looking worried.

'Excuse me, Duchess,' Pow Pow said.

'I can't talk to you right now,' the Duchess replied. 'I'm too **upset** about Nessie.'

'That's why we're here,' I said. 'We're hoping we can **save** the Loch Ness monster by representing East Castle. Will you **allow** it?'

'What makes you think you can **defeat** those West Castle beasts?' the Duchess asked.

'I'm not sure we can,' Pow Pow said. 'But we'd rather **try and fail** than allow the West Coast Warriors to hunt Nessie.'

The Duchess stared at us for what seemed like an eternity. 'I would **love** the six of you to represent my castle,' she said.

Get down there and do us proud!

SiX

When we returned to the clearing, the crowd was packing up to leave. Robert rushed over to Anna and whispered something in her ear.

Anna listened carefully then announced excitedly,

'LADIES AND GENTLEMEN, DON'T LEAVE YOUR SEATS. WE ARE RUMBLING AFTER ALL!'

A murmur spread through the crowd
and then everyone began to **cheer** and
clap.

'We have a **new group** of gladiators representing East Castle,' Anna continued. 'Give it up for Pow Pow Pig, Barry the Goat, Cha Cha Chicken, Kung Fu Duck, Nelson the Pig and Kenny the Goat!'

As we made our way into the clearing, the crowd **cheered** loudly!

'As always,' Anna said, 'the first event, is the *ALL—IN TUG OF WAR!*'

The crowd went **berserk** as both teams grabbed either side of a huge rope.

'One ... two ... three ... HEAVE!' Anna shouted.

We pulled and tugged and heaved with all our might, but the West Castle Warriors were **TOO STRONG** and quickly pulled us over the victory line.

'Tug of war victory in record time,' Anna said, 'goes to the West Castle Warriors!'

The West Castle crowd **ROARED.** The East Castle crowd went dead quiet. The Duchess dropped her head.

'It's just the first event,' Pow Pow said to us all. 'They won that one with strength, but we can win the others with **brains** and **teamwork.**'

We nodded, desperately hoping Pow Pow was right.

'The next challenge,' Anna said, 'is **JOUSTING!**'

The crowd cheered and clapped again.

'Jousting?' Kenny said, scanning the clearing. 'Where are the **horses?**'

'We don't joust with horses,' Anna said. 'We joust on **one another's backs!**'

On the other side of the arena, the crazy-faced raccoon was already mounting the giant lizard.

'Who's up for a little **piggybacking?**' Barry asked. 'Pow Pow?'

'I see what you did there, Barry,' Pow Pow replied with a smile. 'But I vote that **you** piggyback **Nelson.**'

Everyone agreed this sounded like a better combination.

'Me and my **big mouth,**' Barry muttered as I jumped on his back.

'Are we ready to **JOUST?**' Anna shouted.

The crowd replied with a huge roar.

'BRING IT ON!'

Before Barry and I had a chance to gather our thoughts, the raccoon and the lizard **charged** towards us. The raccoon's jousting stick was aimed straight for my head, but I managed to **duck** underneath, narrowly avoiding it!

The lizard and raccoon charged at us over and over. Each time, Barry and I **dodged** the deadly jousting stick.

'We can't keep defending,' Barry said. 'Time to go on the **offence.**'

'I don't do it often,' I said, 'but I can be **offensive** if I need to be!'

The raccoon scrunched up its little face as the giant lizard **thundered** towards us once more.

This time I **didn't** duck. Instead, I used everything I'd learnt as Ninja Kid to knock the jousting stick out of the raccoon's hand.

WHACK

Then I **kicked** the raccoon off the lizard's back.

The East Castle villagers went **WILD!** So did the rest of our team!

WE'D WON!!!

'Congratulations to the East Castle Gladiators,' Anna said. 'The castles are now evenly poised at **ONE ALL.** It's time for . . .

THE MUD BATTLE!'

Pow Pow took on the **giant gorilla** in an epic stick fight above a giant mud pit. The gorilla was **powerful** but thanks to Pow Pow's broom experience, and some **quick thinking,** he came out on top!

YAY!

THUNK!

Next up was a **ROCK-CLIMBING BATTLE.** Cha Cha raced valiantly up the rock face but the West Castle wolf was too **quick** and **cunning.**

Kung Fu Duck battled bravely against the hyena in a KNIGHT FIGHT!

Both were dressed in armour, and went at each other with swords, shields and maces! After an **epic contest,** the hyena bundled Kung Fu out of the fight zone.

'It's time for our **final** challenge,' Anna announced. 'A no holds barred, one-on-one **WRESTLING MATCH.**'

The crowd went **NUTS!**

'Only competitors who have not participated in a challenge can compete,' Anna added. 'That leaves **Kenny** the Goat, and the Duke of West Castle . . .

CONAN THE RHINO!'

Suddenly, Kenny felt nervous. 'Are you **sure** you don't have an angry squirrel over there? Or maybe a **hamster?**' he asked hopefully.

Kenny turned to me, looking a little pale. 'That rhino is **ten times** the size of me,' he said, shaking. 'He looks **TEN TIMES ANGRIER,** too!'

Kenny was right. Conan was **stomping** his feet and **snarling**.

GRRRRRR!

'It's **OK** to be nervous,' Cha Cha said to Kenny. 'But you can **defeat** Conan. Because the strongest doesn't always win. Often, it's the most **skilful**.'

'What skills do I have that could help me wrestle a **giant ANGRY rhino?**' Kenny asked.

'**D & S**,' Cha Cha said.

'What's D & S?' I asked.

DISTRACTION and SURPRISE!

'Kenny and Conan,' Anna announced, 'please step into the clearing.'

Conan **stomped** towards Kenny, a giant club in his hand. Kenny looked over to me with **fear** in his eyes.

'You've got this, Kenny,' I said. **'D & S!'**

'You're right,' Kenny said. 'I'm going to kick that regal **rhino's butt** with D & S! Which stands for . . . umm, **DIRECTION** and . . . **SUPPLIES?!'**

'DISTRACTION and SURPRISE, Kenny! **You've got this!'** said Cha Cha.

'Here, this will help.' Pow Pow handed Kenny his broom.

'let's get ready to rumble!'

Anna shouted.

Conan wasted no time in racing over to Kenny, picking him up, holding him above his head . . .

then throwing him to the ground!

'**Ouch!**' said Kung Fu Duck. 'Got him with the **RHINO-SLAM!**'

'He's forgotten everything I told him,' Cha Cha said.

'Kenny!' I called out. **'D & S!'**

This seemed to flick a switch in Kenny's brain. The next time Conan charged, Kenny said to him, **'Oh, I love this song!'**

This confused Conan. 'What song?' The giant rhino turned his head, trying to hear the imaginary music.

While Conan was **distracted,** Kenny whipped the club out of the rhino's hand and used it to trip Conan over. He went crashing down with an almighty thud!

As he lay there winded, Kenny **pinned** Conan to the ground with the heavy club. Conan tried to free himself from Kenny's surprisingly firm grip, but Anna began the count. **'Three . . . two . . .'**

Conan writhed and kicked but couldn't escape the weight of his club.

'ONE!' Anna exclaimed. Then she held up Kenny's hand. **'We have a WINNER!'**

Kenny couldn't believe it. Cha Cha was so **proud,** she hoisted Kenny onto her shoulders to celebrate!

'**Victory to Kenny,**' Anna said, her voice full of tension and suspense. 'That means this year's battle ...

. . . is a tie!'

The crowd fell **silent,** unsure what would happen next.

'According to ancient law,' Anna continued, studying an old scroll, 'the battle will proceed to a **tie-break round.** This involves the West Castle Warriors attempting to catch the Loch Ness monster and the East Castle Gladiators trying to **stop** them!'

Everyone was stunned.

'I can't believe they're **allowed** to hunt the Loch Ness monster,' Pow Pow said.

'They won't be if we have anything to do with it,' Kung Fu said.

SEVEN

That night, as the **full moon** lit up the sky, we hid in shrubbery near the lake, hoping to **stop** the West Castle Warriors from getting anywhere near Nessie.

We couldn't see any sign of them. But we did see Nessie.

She **popped up** under a giant peach tree and chomped at a juicy peach!

Just as Nessie was about to eat a second peach, the West Castle Warriors emerged from a bush right near the peach tree and threw a **net** over the beautiful creature.

Nessie **thrashed** and **splashed** but the net was too strong and she couldn't break free.

'**let her go,**' Pow Pow shouted from across the lake.

'Why would we do that?' Conan replied smugly, knowing there was nothing we could do to stop them.

Eventually, Nessie gave up fighting and sagged into the net.

The West Castle beasts **cheered** as they tied the net to their huge rowboat and dragged Nessie to the moat surrounding West Castle.

All we could do was watch **helplessly** as they dumped Nessie at the bottom of the moat.

Then they **jumped** off their boat and went into West Castle.

'Poor Nessie,' Barry said, staring at the moat.

'We have to **rescue** her,' Pow Pow said.

'One hundred percent agree,' Cha Cha replied. 'But how? None of us can swim that deep.'

'I can!' Kung Fu said. 'I'm a **duck** after all!'

'Well, take this, you might need it,' said Cha Cha, tossing Kung Fu her **Mixy-Fixy,** the amazing all-in-one tool she always carried.

'I'll come with you,' I said.

'How will you hold your breath that long?' Barry asked. 'You're just a pig . . . I mean, a human dressed as a pig.'

'With **this,** I said, gesturing to my underwater necklace.

'Nessie's future **depends** on you,'
Pow Pow said to me and Kung Fu as we
prepared to head underwater.

'Good luck, **little gladiators,**' Cha
Cha said.

'Thanks,' I replied.

Then Kung Fu and I **dived** into the
moat.

The water was **murky** at first. We could barely see our hands in front of us as we swam.

But it cleared up the further we swam, and then we saw her . . .

. . . the mighty Loch Ness monster.
She looked anything but mighty as she
lay **trapped** at the bottom of the moat.

Kung Fu Duck cut Nessie **free** from the net using the Mixy-Fixy. Then we rolled three rocks into the net to trick the West Castle Warriors into thinking Nessie was still **trapped** at the bottom of the moat.

'Thank you so much,' Nessie said. 'How can I ever **repay** you?'

'You could give us a **lift** back to our friends,' Kung Fu said.

'That's the least I could do!' Nessie said. 'Hang on tight, because you're in for the **ride of your life!**'

We jumped on Nessie's back and she **RACED** through the water. It was like the world's best water-park ride as we rode the Loch Ness monster through the lake, careful not to attract the attention of anyone from West Castle.

Nessie returned us to the edge of the lake where Kenny, Pow Pow, Barry and Cha Cha were waiting with the Duchess. The Duchess was so **relieved** that Nessie was OK she wept with joy.

'Hey, Nessie,' I said, still on the giant creature's back, 'do you remember taking a **funny-looking camera** yesterday?'

'Of course I do!' Nessie said excitedly.

'Can we please have the camera back?' I asked.

'Of course,' Nessie replied. 'It's in my cave. Climb aboard, everyone, I'll take you there!'

Nessie ferried us through the water, eventually stopping at a small **island** in the middle of the lake.

'My cave is down there,' she pointed to the depths below. 'I know Nelson and Kung Fu are excellent at holding their breath, but what about the rest of you?'

'We're strictly **land creatures,**' Pow Pow said. 'We'll wait up here!'

'I would dearly love to see your cave,' the Duchess said. 'But I'm **terrible** at holding my breath.'

'Here,' Kenny said, handing the Duchess his underwater necklace. 'You can stay underwater as long as you like with this.'

'Thank you so much, Kenny,' the Duchess said, studying the necklace.

Nessie left the rest of us on the small island then dived underwater with the Duchess.

When they resurfaced, the Duchess was gushing. 'That was the most **beautiful** thing I've ever seen. And look who I met.'

A male Loch Ness monster popped his head out of the water. And he was piggybacking a **BABY** monster!

'Gang,' Nessie said. 'Meet my husband, Nate, and my little girl, Nikki.'

It was only now that I noticed Nikki had something between her lips. Something **very important** to me and Kenny!

Nate looked to his daughter. 'Nikki, it's time to give the camera back, OK?'

The baby Loch Ness monster shook her little head.

'Sweetheart,' Nessie said gently. 'The camera doesn't belong to you. How would you feel if someone took one of your toys?'

The baby looked at her mum, then at her dad. Then she handed me the camera. **'Thank you,** little one,' I said to Nikki, who smiled and **giggled.**

'Unfortunately, I need to head back to the castle for official duties,' the Duchess said.

'I'll take you all there,' Nessie said. 'Everyone, **hop back on!**'

We jumped on Nessie's back and went for another water ride to East Castle.

After we dismounted Nessie, the beautiful creature gave us a **wink** and a smile then disappeared under the water.

'Thanks for saving our beautiful monsters,' the Duchess said to us. 'And thanks for letting me **borrow** this.'

She moved to hand Kenny the underwater necklace.

'Keep it, Duchess,' Kenny said. 'Then you can **visit** Nessie and her family whenever you like.'

'And **warn them** if the West Castle Warriors are approaching,' I said.

'That's the most **brilliant** present I've ever received!' the Duchess said. 'Thank you!'

She wrapped Kenny in an enormous hug.

The Duchess bade us farewell and headed for the castle. Once she was out of sight, Cha Cha pulled back some shrubbery to reveal their **Time Machine.**

'Whoa!' Kenny exclaimed. 'That looks even **cooler** than in the books!'

'It would be cool if it actually took us to the year we **wanted** to go to!' Kung Fu said.

'I think it just needs a little more **tinkering**,' Cha Cha said as she began making adjustments with her Mixy-Fixy.

As Cha Cha made her repairs, Barry turned towards us. 'Can you boys get back home?' he asked.

'I think so!' I said, looking **hopefully** at the Character Camera.

'Awesome teamwork, boys,' Pow Pow said.

'You, too,' I replied.

We all hugged and said our farewells.

'Hopefully, we'll see each other again **super soon,** Cha Cha said.

I pointed the Character Camera at me and Kenny. 'Say: Homecoming!'

Next thing we knew, Kenny and I were back in our bedroom!

'That was **intense**,' I exclaimed.

'Good intense!' Kenny said.

'**GREAT intense**,' I said. 'And now I know exactly what we should **paint** for the art competition!'

The Loch Ness monster!

EiGHT

Kenny and **I** made sure to dress the part for the art exhibition.

Sarah and Tiffany were also dressed to **impress.**

We were all **super pumped** about seeing our artworks in the Town Hall. The first thing we noticed when we walked in were two **HUGE STATUES.**

'Who made these?' I asked Mr Fletcher.

'Mocasso,' Mr Fletcher replied.

It didn't take long for Tiffany and Sarah to find their artwork. It was AWESOME!

Then we showed the girls our creation . . .

'It's beautiful,' Sarah said.

'Where did you get your **inspiration?**'
Tiffany asked.

'Ah . . . we had a **dream** about it,' I said.
'It was such a **vivid dream,** it felt
like we really met her!' Kenny added.

The other kids' paintings were also
AMAZING.

Charles had done a painting of **himself** as a **mythical beast** with wings and a tail!

Billy Bob's painting was of his llama, Wally, with the **Mona Lisa's face!**

'I'm impressed by all of your artworks,' Mr Fletcher said as he wandered around the room.

'But it's not **your opinion** that matters,' Mocasso said as he glided towards a podium in the middle of the gallery. 'Children, gather around.'

We did as **Mocasso** asked, sitting in chairs he had arranged around the podium.

'I have had a long, hard look at your creations,' Mocasso said. 'And it's time to announce the **winner** of my fabulously *fancy* art prize.'

'I'm only now realising how much I want this,' I whispered to Kenny.

'Me too,' Kenny replied.

We were all on the edge of our **seats!**

'The winner is . . .' Mocasso said in his most dramatic voice. We all leaned further forward.

'**Nobody!**' Mocasso announced. 'Because you're all **LOSERS! HA!**'

Then Mocasso pulled at his face and ripped off a **MASK!**

It was **DR KANE!**

Our first reaction was **ANGER.**
We'd put so much effort into our art
projects. All for a **fake competition!**

But there was no time to wallow,
because now we were in serious danger.

'**Attack!**' Dr Kane yelled.

Our anger turned to fear when the
centaur and Cyclops came to life and

STORMED TOWARDS US!

As the centaur galloped on his horse legs, he waved a sharp **spear** above his human head.

The Cyclops was brandishing a large wooden **club** as it **STOMPED** towards us with its tree-trunk legs.

It was already pure **CHAOS** when Dr Kane's sidekick, Einstein the wisecracking chipmunk, came flying into the room in his helicopter. 'This is **my kind** of art show!' he yelled excitedly.

WHOOSH!

'Run for your lives!' Charles screamed as he bolted for the door.

Mr Fletcher and the rest of the class followed him.

Dr Kane and Einstein laughed like maniacs.

'It's a pity your artwork isn't as good as your **RUNNING!**' Einstein cackled.

'Tell your parents to run, too!' Dr Kane yelled. 'And your siblings. And your grandparents. **This is my town now!'**

Sarah, Tiffany, Kenny and I were the only kids left in the hall. The centaur and Cyclops were headed **straight for us!**

'Follow the others,' I said to Sarah and Tiffany. 'Kenny and I will **rescue** the paintings.'

'We'll help you,' Tiffany said.

The centaur charged at us with its spear. The Cyclops raised its club, ready to **strike.**

'Our paintings are great,' Sarah said, 'but they're not worth **fighting** these two over. We ALL need to get out of here. **NOW!**'

She raced out of the hall and Tiffany followed. Kenny and I hesitated.

'Guys!' Sarah exclaimed. 'Come on!'

Kenny and I **rushed** out of the Town Hall. As soon as Sarah and Tiffany blended into the crowd, we **snuck back** into the hall.

As Dr Kane and Einstein **congratulated** themselves on kicking everyone out of town, Kenny and I quietly crawled under the tables towards the Town Hall bathroom.

NiNE

When we emerged from the bathroom, we were **NiNJA** and **KiD** **H-DUDE!**

'Wait a second!' Dr Kane said when he saw us. 'Where did you **dweebs** come from?'

'That's our little secret,' Kenny replied.

'I also have a secret,' Dr Kane said. 'You're both about to **perish!**' He turned to the Cyclops and centaur in a rage. **'Pulverise them!'**

'Yeah!' Einstein said. 'Pulverise them!'

'No need to **repeat** what I say!' Dr Kane snapped at Einstein.

The centaur and Cyclops didn't care about Dr Kane and Einstein's bickering. They were focused on annihilating us.

The centaur lunged at us with its **SSS (Super Sharp Spear!)**.

'Jump!' I shouted to Kenny.

'JUMPING!' Kenny replied.

We leapt as high as we could, narrowly avoiding the tip of the centaur's spear.

The fact we avoided the spear was the **good** news. The fact we landed right in front of the club-wielding Cyclops was **the BAD news!**

It stared at us with its one menacing eye. Then, before Kenny and I had time to **escape,** it picked Kenny up with one giant hand and me with the other and banged us together like we were **COCONUTS.**

CLUNK!

Dr Kane and Einstein **cackled** with laughter, which made our heads hurt even more.

And the **pain** was far from over.

The centaur kicked its powerful legs out behind, sending us **flying across the room!**

KICK!

WHOA!

Dr Kane and Einstein **screamed** with joy.

'This fight is really **KICKING OFF!**' Dr Kane said.

'I never want it to end!' Einstein agreed.

'I think we've finally met our match, Ninja Kid,' Kenny said rubbing his head.

'There must be some way we can **stop** them,' I replied.

Then Kenny remembered something he learnt off Cha Cha Chicken. 'I have an idea!' he said excitedly. '**DISTRACT** and **SURPRISE!**'

'Now you're talking!' I whispered. 'You take the D. I've got the S.'

It's DISTRACT o'clock!

'Hey guys, look over here!' said Kenny. 'You can come and get me, if you know which way I'm going!'

Then Kenny started to do the **MOONWALK!**

The Cyclops and the centaur stared at him in **confusion.**

'What are you waiting for?' Dr Kane bellowed. **'Finish him!'**

'Yeah, finish him,' Einstein repeated.

The centaur and Cyclops raced after Kenny, who **DISTRACTED** them by bursting into song as he slid backwards across the floor!

But I couldn't think of a **SURPRISE!**

The centaur was trying to **THUMP** Kenny, but Kenny's moves confused it and the centaur was wrong-footed. It **SMASHED** its right leg on a table. Then a **strange** thing happened . . . sparks burst out of the centaur's leg!

FiZZ!

'They're **ROBOTS!**' I shouted to Kenny. 'Good for them!' Kenny said as he dodged and weaved the centaur.

Knowing they were **robots** gave me the opportunity for **surprise** that I was looking for. I raced to the bathroom and returned with a bucket.

'Cyclops! Centaur! How about a little **SLIP AND SLIDE?**'

The Cyclops and centaur grunted angrily then **rushed** towards me.

When they got close, I hurled the bucket of water at them. The Cyclops and centaur **SLIPPED** and **SPARKED** . . . then burst into flames!

SPLASH!

'**Nooooo!**' Dr Kane groaned.

'Stop bursting into flames, stupid robots!' Einstein yelled.

I looked at Dr Kane, anger swelling in my throat. Then I grabbed the centaur's spear and used it to pin Dr Kane to the wall.

Dr Kane had no idea who I was under my mask.

'Where's the **ULTIMATE NINJA?'** I asked.

Despite the spear trapping him, Dr Kane remained cool. 'He's back in training,' he said. 'The next time you see him will be when he defeats you!'

Dr Kane's mocking tone made me even **ANGRIER.** But before I could do anything, Einstein threw a grappling hook out of his helicopter.

I looked up in **surprise,** and Dr Kane pushed the spear aside, grabbing the hook. With one last laugh, he whirled away as Einstein **lifted** him out of the hall.

'You lose again, **Whinge-y Kid** and **Lame Dude!**' Dr Kane yelled down to us.

'Funny,' I said. 'I don't feel like a **loser.**'

'Yeah,' Kenny added. 'You're the ones **running away.**'

'Because we kicked your butts!' I said.

When the other kids saw that Dr Kane and Einstein were **leaving,** they headed back into the Town Hall. Kenny and I raced to the bathroom and quickly **changed** out of our costumes. Then we snuck out of the hall and doubled back, **pretending** to be returning with the other kids.

Sarah and Tiffany caught up to us inside.

'I wonder what made Dr Kane leave in such a hurry?' Sarah asked.

'Yeah,' Tiffany said. 'And what happened to his **scary sculptures?**' She studied the Cyclops and centaur, which were banged up and scorched on the floor.

It was then that I had a horrible realisation: I had changed out of my costume so quickly that my **mask** was **sticking out of my pants!**

'Hey, check this out!' I said, throwing the mask on the ground and pretending to discover it. 'Looks like **NiNJA KiD** and **H-DUDE** were here!'

'Where would this town be without them?!' Kenny added, hiding a smile.

'I can't believe they didn't say hi to us,' Tiffany said.

'They probably had their **hands full** with that creepy Cyclops and centaur,' Sarah replied.

'Yeah. It must be a full-time job for them being that **skilful** and **handsome**,' Kenny said.

TEN

When we arrived home, Kenny and I told Mum and Grandma about our **crazy** day. Firstly, being transported into the world of Pow Pow Pig, then coming face to face with Dr Kane and his robotic mythical beasts.

'Today is the **ANGRIEST** I've ever felt towards Dr Kane,' I said.

I looked to Mum and Grandma. 'Next
time I see the Ultimate Ninja, I'm going to
free Dad from Dr Kane's evil control and
bring him home.'

'That would be **incredible**,' Mum said
hopefully.

'Oh, and I have something to **confess**,' Kenny said to Grandma.

'Yes, Kenny?' Grandma asked warily.

'**I gave away** one of your inventions,' Kenny replied.

Grandma almost **choked** on her spaghetti.

'You gave away one of my inventions?!' Grandma exclaimed. 'Which one? And to who?'

'I gave my underwater necklace to the Duchess,' Kenny said. 'So she can visit the Loch Ness monster's cave whenever she likes.'

'And warn her of any **danger**,' I added.

'She was super excited about it,' Kenny said.

'That sounds like a **lovely** gesture,' Grandma said. 'But you need to be more careful with the Character Camera. No more using it on each other.'

'Sounds fair,' I said.

'**Super fair**,' Kenny agreed, through a mouthful of spaghetti.

'There's one **final mystery** to be solved,' I said.

'What's that?' Kenny asked.

'Who bought us the *Pow Pow Pig* book?' I said.

Mum and Grandma started **laughing.**

'We bought it for you,' Mum said.

'You two are not the only ones allowed to have **secrets,**' Grandma said.

'Then you're both entitled to one **free Kenny hug!**' Kenny said.

'And a **Nelson hug,** too!' I said.

READ THEM ALL!

NINJA KID 13 COMING SOON!